Brother and Sister Bear's Internet Rules for Cubs

1. Never give out private information online, such as your address, your phone number, or the name of your school.

2. Tell your parents right away if you see or learn anything online that scares or worries you.

3. Never agree to get together with anyone you "meet" online.

4. Never send your picture or anything else to someone online without your parents' permission.

5. Never answer messages online that make you feel scared or worried.

6. Talk with your parents about rules for going online.

7. Never give out your password to anyone except your parents.

8. Never do anything online that could hurt others.

The Berenstain Bears'
COMPUTER TROUBLE

Computers have their uses—
they're great for work or play.
But it's not a good idea
just to stare at them all day!

The Berenstain Bears' COMPUTER TROUBLE

Jan & Mike Berenstain

HARPER FESTIVAL

An Imprint of HarperCollinsPublishers

The Berenstain Bears' Computer Trouble

Copyright © 2010 by Berenstain Bears, Inc.

HarperFestival is an imprint of HarperCollins Publishers.

www.harpercollinschildrens.com

Library of Congress catalog card number: 2010923281

ISBN 978-0-06-057410-9 (trade bdg.)—ISBN 978-0-06-057394-2 (pbk.)

18 19 20   SCP   10 9 8 7 6 5

❖

First Edition

It was Papa Bear who first brought a computer home to the Bear family's tree house. He thought it would be useful in his furniture business. It did come in handy for printing bills for his customers and doing his taxes.

But Papa soon found that Brother and Sister were coming into his shop to play video games on his computer. Before long they needed their own computers for schoolwork. Email, websites, IMing, and social networking followed.

Mama discovered buying and selling things on e-Bear and wanted a computer, too. Even Honey Bear began playing simple computer games on a toy computer. Now it seemed to Papa that the whole family spent most of their time in front of computers every day from early morning until late at night.

Though it was Papa who first got the computer, it was Papa who finally had enough. His business was making things out of wood. He loved wood. He loved working with his hands. But he did not love sitting in front of a computer. One afternoon, he came in from his shop with a headache from staring at the computer too long.

"Hello!" he called. "Is anybody home? Where is everyone?" He headed upstairs looking for someone to talk to. He came to Sister's room. To his surprise, he found Sister with her head down on her desk, crying her eyes out.

"Whatever is wrong, dear?" asked Papa, patting her back. "What on earth happened?"

"It's my stupid Pawbook webpage!"
Sister sobbed. "That awful Billy Grizzwold
wrote on it that I'm a 'fuzzy-faced hair
ball' for all my friends to see and
now they're saying we're in *love*!"
She burst into a fresh fountain of
tears.

Papa rolled his eyes.
Computers, he thought. *Nothing
but trouble!*

"Come on," he said. "Let's figure out how to deal with this on your Pawbook page."

Then Papa noticed loud music coming from Brother's room. He went next door and found Brother playing music on his computer while looking at soccer gear on a website.

"Aren't you supposed to be doing your homework?" asked Papa.
"Don't worry, Papa," said Brother, "I'm working on it in between
checking out websites—see?" He clicked his mouse and showed Papa his
homework on the screen.

Papa rolled his eyes again as Sister called him back to her room. He peeked into Honey's room across the hall. Even she was playing a game on her computer. Farther down the hall, Papa could see Mama at her computer, too. Then the doorbell rang.

"Can you get that, dear?" called Mama. "I'm busy bidding on something on e-Bear."

DING DONG!

Wearily, Papa headed downstairs. It was Herb the mailman, with a package.

"Thanks, Herb," said Papa, signing for it. He noticed the package was from e-Bear.

"You know, Papa," said Herb, "you've got to get this e-Bear thing with Mama under control. This is the fifth package this week. You're going to go broke. See you later!"

Papa rolled his eyes yet again. *More computer trouble!* He decided that instead of just rolling his eyes he was going to do something about it. That evening, after dinner, Papa made an announcement.

"I believe that this family is having computer trouble," said Papa.
Everyone looked at him in surprise.
"What sort of trouble?" asked Mama.
"We are having trouble with email, websites, Pawbook, computer games, and e-Bear," Papa said, folding his arms. "We are spending so much time on computers that we don't even have time to say hello to each other these days."

Mama had been worrying about this very thing herself. She just didn't seem to be able to tear herself away from e-Bear.

"Well," she said, "what are we going to do about it?"

"It seems to me," explained Papa, "that the big problem is the internet. It takes up too much time, gets us to spend too much money, and it can be dangerous! Here, look at this." He showed them the evening newspaper. "Internet Child Safety Problems," said the headline. "It says here that people use the internet to get cubs to do things that aren't safe."

"I guess we do need to have rules for the cubs about the internet," agreed Mama.

"And I'm going to turn the internet off except for one hour each day," added Papa.

"Only one hour?" said the cubs.

"That's plenty," said Papa. "If you can't get done what you need to do on the internet in one hour, it's not worth doing."

"But what will we do instead?" asked Brother.

"You can get back outside and play like you used to," said Papa. "You can play ball, go skateboarding, ride your bikes, fly kites, go fishing, go for a five-mile hike, pick wildflowers, watch clouds, walk the dog, play with kittens, collect rocks, pretend you're space bears, run around in circles and get dizzy, make mud pies, catch bugs, chase each other, and scream!"

Sister and Brother giggled.
It sounded like fun.

After school the next day, Brother and Sister did get outside to play like they used to. It was so much fun that they went over to Cousin Fred's and Lizzy Bruin's to get them to leave their computers and come outside, too. They all went down to the playground for some good old-fashioned exercise on the good old-fashioned swings, seesaws, jungle gyms, slides, and the merry-go-round.

After dinner that evening, Brother and Sister went online for just one hour and were surprised to find it was plenty of time after all.

Papa learned he didn't need to waste so much time online to get his business done. He was able to stay in his shop working with the wood he loved.

Freed from the spell of e-Bear, Mama got out her old quilting kit and started work on a big quilt of birds and butterflies. She got so involved that she didn't go online for even one hour.

When the internet hour was over, the Bear family
gathered together in front of the fireplace in the living room.
They sat and read for a while. Mama did some knitting. And
then, wonder of wonders, they began to talk. They talked
about all kinds of things.

They talked about what happened in school that day, about how Billy Grizzwold apologized for calling Sister a "fuzzy-faced hair ball." They talked about Brother's soccer practice after school and the terrific corner kick he'd bent into the goal.

Mama told them about her plans for making beautiful new quilts, and Papa told them how he had really gotten into that new batch of curly maple he had in the shop. Finally, all tired out, they got ready for bed.

The next evening, the Bear family decided that they didn't want to stay home sitting in front of a computer screen at all. They did wind up sitting in front of a screen that evening, but it was a much, much bigger one and they got to eat popcorn, too. While Grizzly Gramps and Gran took care of Honey, they all went out to the movies.

"What will it be?" asked Papa, buying the tickets. "*Pirates of the Bearibbean*, *Beary Potter*, or *Spider-Bear*?"

"*Spider-Bear*!" they all agreed.

And *Spider-Bear* it was.